Rookie reader

the Secret Code

written by
Dana Meachen Rau

illustrated by
Bari Weissman

Children's Press ®
A Division of Grolier Publishing
New York • London • Hong Kong • Sydney
Danbury, Connecticut

For Derek, who sees more than I ever will —D. M. R.

To my beloved Ida, the sweetest dog ever —B. W.

Reading Consultant
Linda Cornwell
Learning Resource Consultant, Indiana Department of Education

AUTHOR'S NOTE:

Blind people are not able to read books the same way many people do, because they cannot see with their eyes. So in 1829, Louis Braille, a blind French student, published a simple code based on a system of six raised dots (⠿). He made it possible for blind people to read by touch.

On pages 22 and 23, you can see that the letters of the Braille alphabet are different combinations of these six dots. Check your local library for a Braille book that you can feel on your own!

Visit Children's Press® on the Internet at:
http://publishing.grolier.com

Library of Congress Cataloging-in-Publication Data
Rau, Dana Meachen, 1971–
The secret code / by Dana Meachen Rau ; illustrated by Bari Weissman.
p. cm. —(A rookie reader)
Summary: Oscar, who is blind, teaches Lucy how to read his Braille book.
ISBN 0-516-20700-8 (lib. bdg.)   0-516-26362-5 (pbk.)
[1. Braille—Fiction. 2. Blind—Fiction. 3. Physically handicapped—Fiction.]
I. Weissman, Bari, ill. II. Title. III. Series.
PZ7.R193975Sh 1998
[E] —dc21   97-18797
                                                               CIP
                                                                AC

19 20 21 22 R 21 20 19 18   62

Scholastic Inc., 557 Broadway, New York, NY 10012.

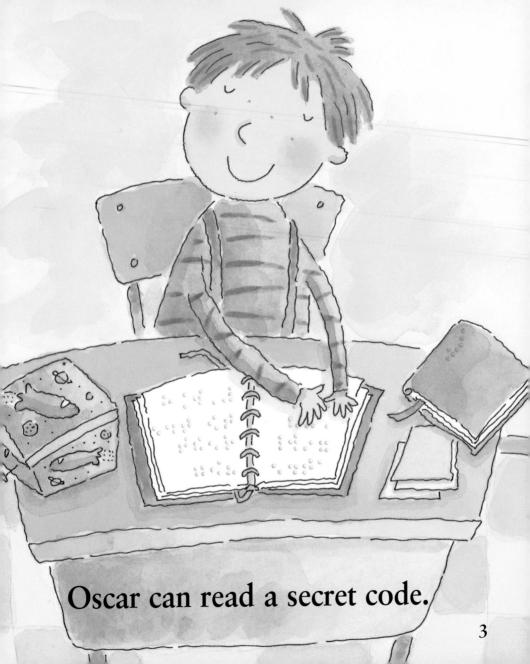

Oscar can read a secret code.

Lucy saw it when Oscar
opened his book.

4

Oscar's book
is different from Lucy's.

Lucy's page has black letters.
She reads with her eyes.

The girl and her dog ran and ran and ran as fast as they could go.

Oscar's page is covered with bumps.
He reads with his fingers!

LIBRARY →

12

"Is that a secret code?" Lucy asks.
"It's not a secret! It's Braille!"
Oscar says. "I can teach it to you."

14

Each set of bumps is a letter.
Together, they form words.

"Just like my letters!" Lucy says.

Oscar is blind,
so he doesn't see the letters.
He feels them.

When Lucy learns a b c,
Oscar learns .

a b c d e

f g h i j

k l m n o

p q r s t

u v w x y

z capital
sign period

Now Lucy knows the secret code.

25

Oscar can write notes to Lucy . . .

. . . and Lucy can read the message.

31

Word List (69 words)

a	from	Lucy's	set
and	fun	message	she
asks	has	my	so
black	he	not	teach
blind	her	notes	that
book	his	now	the
Braille	I	of	them
bumps	is	opened	they
can	isn't	Oscar	to
code	it	Oscar's	together
covered	it's	page	when
different	just	read	with
doesn't	knows	reading	words
each	learns	reads	write
eyes	letter	saw	you
feels	letters	says	
fingers	like	secret	
form	Lucy	see	

About the Author

Dana Meachen Rau is the author of many books for children. She also works as a children's book editor and lives with her husband, Chris, in Southbury, Connecticut. Dana's brother, Derek, is blind. When they were kids, Derek taught Dana how to read Braille. (She reads it with her eyes, not her fingers!) Dana has always been impressed by, and often boasts about, her brother's ability to read in the dark!

About the Illustrator

Bari Weissman has illustrated approximately twenty children's books in her twenty-year career. To research Braille for this book, she visited Perkins School for the Blind in Massachusetts and looked at the Braille books there. Bari lives in Boston, Massachusetts with her husband, Warren, and their cat, Ishkabbible.